PADDINGTON

Library of Congress catalog card number: 2014934801
ISBN 978-0-06-231720-9

15   16   17   18   19   SCP   10   9   8   7   6   5   4   3   2   1
❖
First US edition, 2009

Originally published in Great Britain by HarperCollins Children's Books as
Paddington Rules the Waves in 2008

MICHAEL BOND

PADDINGTON

AT THE BEACH

illustrated by R. W. ALLEY

HARPER
An Imprint of HarperCollinsPublishers

Nothing much goes on at the seaside that
seagulls don't know about.
So when Paddington went down to the beach
early one morning, he soon had company.

"It's a bear," cried seagull number 1,
"and he's digging up our beach!"

"He's made a sand castle,"
said seagull number 2.
"Look how pleased he is."

"Now he's lost his bucket," said
seagull number 3.
"I could have told him that would
happen. *Screech! Screech!*"

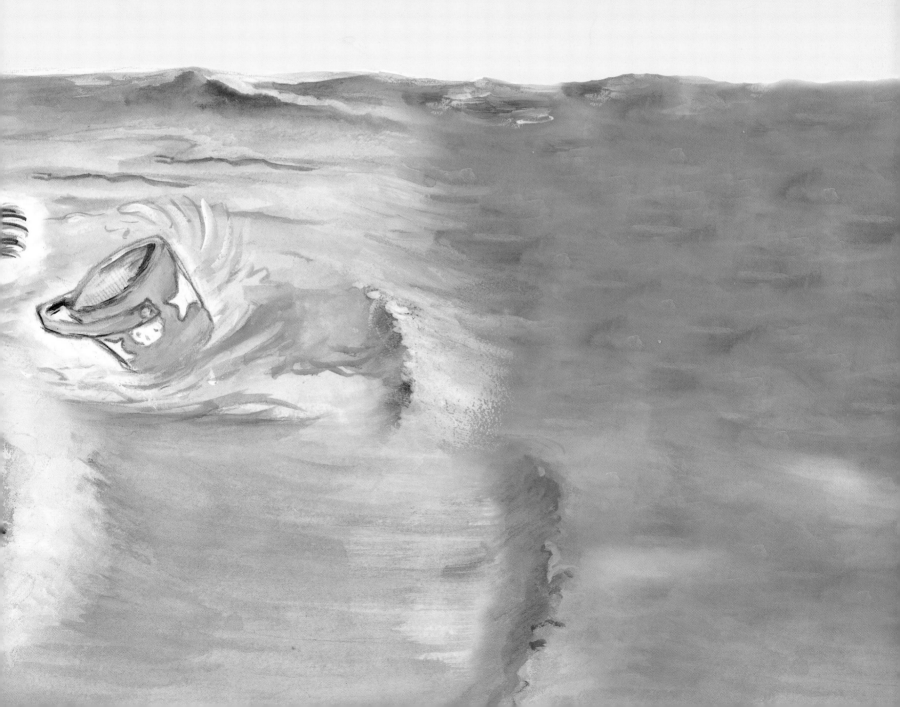

"I think he must be learning to fly,"
said seagull number 4 as Paddington
began playing with his kite.

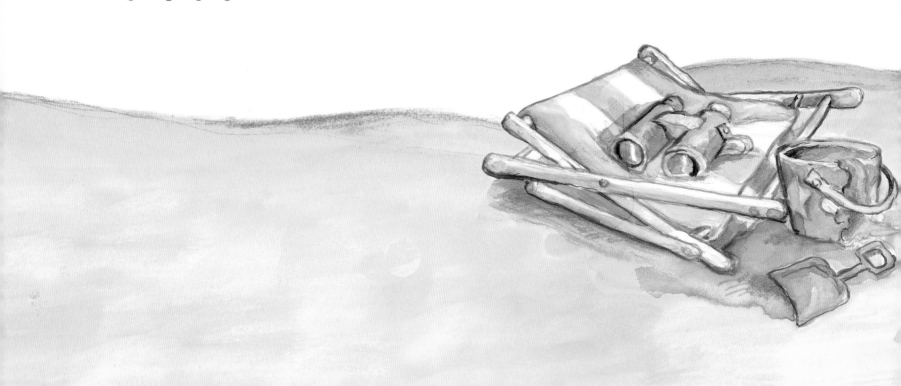

"He's much too heavy for that,"
screeched seagull number 5.

"What did I tell you?" it cried, as
seagull number 6 joined them.

As Paddington was looking out to sea
for his kite, seagull number 7 flew in.
"Look!" it cried.
"He's got a bun in his pocket!"

While Paddington struggled with his
deck chair, seagull number 8 landed.
"I'm hungry," it screeched. "Shall I
try giving the bun a peck and see what
happens?"

"Wait until there are more of us,"
hissed seagull number 9.

Sure enough, a moment later, seagull
number 10 arrived.
"Here goes!" called one at the back.
And they all made a dive.

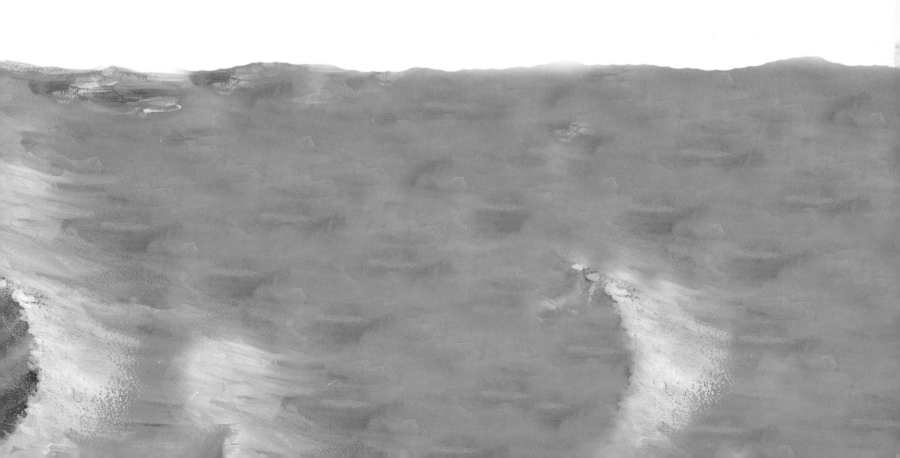

"Seagulls don't know everything," said
Paddington when they had gone.
"I always keep a marmalade sandwich
under my hat, just in case!"